Guy de Maupassant's Tales of Revenge

-

A Collection of
Short Stories

British Library Cataloguing-in-Publication Data
A catalogue record for this book is available from the
British Library

Contents

Guy De Maupassant

Henri-René-Albert-Guy de Maupassant was born in 1850 at the Château de Miromesnil, near Dieppe, France. He came from a prosperous family, but when Maupassant was eleven, his mother risked social disgrace by trying to secure a legal separation from her husband. After the split, Maupassant lived with his mother till he was thirteen, and inherited her love of classical literature, especially Shakespeare. Upon entering high school, he met the great author Gustave Flaubert, and despite being something of an unruly student proved himself as a good scholar, delighting in poetry and theatre.

Not long after he graduated from college in 1870, the Franco-Prussian War broke out, and Maupassant enlisted voluntarily. Afterwards, he moved to Paris, where he spent ten years as a clerk in the Navy Department, and began to write fiction under the guidance of Flaubert. At Flaubert's home he met a number of distinguished authors, including Émile Zola and Ivan Turgenev. In 1878, Maupassant became a contributing editor of several major newspapers, including Le Figaro, Gil Blas, Le Gaulois and l'Écho de Paris, writing fiction in his spare time.

In 1880, Maupassant published his first – and, according to many, his best – short story, entitled 'Boule de Suif' ('Ball of Fat'). It was an instant success. He went on to be extremely prolific during the 1880s, working methodically to produce up to four volumes of short fiction every year. In 1883 and 1885 respectively, Maupassant published Une Vie (A Woman's Life) and Bel-Ami, both of which rank among his best-known works. In 1887, by then a very famous and very wealthy literary figure, he published what is widely regarded as his finest novel, Pierre et Jean.

As well as being a well-known opponent of the construction of the Eiffel Tower, Maupassant was a solitary, withdrawn man with an aversion to public life. In his later years, as a result of the syphilis he had contracted earlier in life, he developed a powerful fear of death and became deeply paranoid. In early 1892, Maupassant tried to commit suicide by cutting his throat, and was committed to a private asylum in Paris. He died here some eighteen months later, aged 42. He penned his own epitaph: "I have coveted everything and taken pleasure in nothing." Some years later, in his autobiography, Friedrich Nietzsche called Maupassant "one of the stronger race, a genuine Latin to whom I am particularly attached."

A Vendetta

The widow of Paolo Saverini lived alone with her son in a poor little house on the outskirts of Bonifacio. The town, built on an outjutting part of the mountain, in places even overhanging the sea, looks across the straits, full of sandbanks, towards the southernmost coast of Sardinia. Beneath it, on the other side and almost surrounding it, is a cleft in the cliff like an immense corridor which serves as a harbor, and along it the little Italian and Sardinian fishing boats come by a circuitous route between precipitous cliffs as far as the first houses, and every two weeks the old, wheezy steamer which makes the trip to Ajaccio.

On the white mountain the houses, massed together, makes an even whiter spot. They look like the nests of wild birds, clinging to this peak, overlooking this terrible passage, where vessels rarely venture. The wind, which blows uninterruptedly, has swept bare the forbidding coast; it drives through the narrow straits and lays waste both sides. The pale streaks of foam, clinging to the black rocks, whose countless peaks rise up out of the water, look like bits of rag floating and drifting on the surface of the sea.

The house of widow Saverini, clinging to the very edge of the precipice, looks out, through its three windows, over this wild and desolate picture.

She lived there alone, with her son Antonia and their dog "Semillante," a big, thin beast, with a long rough coat, of the sheep-dog breed. The young man took her with him when out hunting.

One night, after some kind of a quarrel, Antoine Saverini was treacherously stabbed by Nicolas Ravolati, who escaped the same evening to Sardinia.

When the old mother received the body of her child, which the neighbors had brought back to her, she did not cry, but she stayed there for a long time motionless, watching him. Then, stretching her wrinkled hand over the body, she promised him a vendetta. She did not wish anybody near her, and she shut herself up beside the body with the dog, which howled continuously, standing at the foot of the bed, her head stretched towards her master and her tail between her legs. She did not move any more than did the mother, who, now leaning over the body with a blank stare, was weeping silently and watching it.

The young man, lying on his back, dressed in his jacket of coarse cloth, torn at the chest, seemed to be asleep. But he had blood all over him; on his shirt, which had been torn off in order to administer the first aid; on his vest, on his trousers, on his face, on his hands. Clots of blood had hardened in his beard and in his hair.

His old mother began to talk to him. At the sound of this voice the dog quieted down.

"Never fear, my boy, my little baby, you shall be avenged. Sleep, sleep; you shall be avenged. Do you hear? It's your mother's promise! And she always keeps her word, your mother does, you know she does."

Slowly she leaned over him, pressing her cold lips to his

dead ones.

Then Semillante began to howl again with a long, monotonous, penetrating, horrible howl.

The two of them, the woman and the dog, remained there until morning.

Antoine Saverini was buried the next day and soon his name ceased to be mentioned in Bonifacio.

He had neither brothers nor cousins. No man was there to carry on the vendetta. His mother, the old woman, alone pondered over it.

On the other side of the straits she saw, from morning until night, a little white speck on the coast. It was the little Sardinian village Longosardo, where Corsican criminals take refuge when they are too closely pursued. They compose almost the entire population of this hamlet, opposite their native island, awaiting the time to return, to go back to the "maquis." She knew that Nicolas Ravolati had sought refuge in this village.

All alone, all day long, seated at her window, she was looking over there and thinking of revenge. How could she do anything without help—she, an invalid and so near death? But she had promised, she had sworn on the body. She could not forget, she could not wait. What could she do? She no longer slept at night; she had neither rest nor peace of mind; she thought persistently. The dog, dozing at her feet, would sometimes lift her head and howl. Since her master's death she often howled thus, as though she were calling him, as though her beast's soul, inconsolable too, had also retained a recollection that nothing could wipe out.

One night, as Semillante began to howl, the mother suddenly got hold of an idea, a savage, vindictive, fierce idea. She thought it over until morning. Then, having arisen at daybreak she went to church. She prayed, prostrate on the floor, begging the Lord to help her, to support her, to give to her poor, broken-down body the strength which she needed in order to avenge her son.

She returned home. In her yard she had an old barrel, which acted as a cistern. She turned it over, emptied it, made it fast to the ground with sticks and stones. Then she chained Semillante to this improvised kennel and went into the house.

She walked ceaselessly now, her eyes always fixed on the distant coast of Sardinia. He was over there, the murderer.

All day and all night the dog howled. In the morning the old woman brought her some water in a bowl, but nothing more; no soup, no bread.

Another day went by. Semillante, exhausted, was sleeping. The following day her eyes were shining, her hair on end and she was pulling wildly at her chain.

All this day the old woman gave her nothing to eat. The beast, furious, was barking hoarsely. Another night went by.

Then, at daybreak, Mother Saverini asked a neighbor for some straw. She took the old rags which had formerly been worn by her husband and stuffed them so as to make them look like a human body.

Having planted a stick in the ground, in front of

Semillante's kennel, she tied to it this dummy, which seemed to be standing up. Then she made a head out of some old rags.

The dog, surprised, was watching this straw man, and was quiet, although famished. Then the old woman went to the store and bought a piece of black sausage. When she got home she started a fire in the yard, near the kennel, and cooked the sausage. Semillante, frantic, was jumping about, frothing at the mouth, her eyes fixed on the food, the odor of which went right to her stomach.

Then the mother made of the smoking sausage a necktie for the dummy. She tied it very tight around the neck with string, and when she had finished she untied the dog.

With one leap the beast jumped at the dummy's throat, and with her paws on its shoulders she began to tear at it. She would fall back with a piece of food in her mouth, then would jump again, sinking her fangs into the string, and snatching few pieces of meat she would fall back again and once more spring forward. She was tearing up the face with her teeth and the whole neck was in tatters.

The old woman, motionless and silent, was watching eagerly. Then she chained the beast up again, made her fast for two more days and began this strange performance again.

For three months she accustomed her to this battle, to this meal conquered by a fight. She no longer chained her up, but just pointed to the dummy.

She had taught her to tear him up and to devour him without even leaving any traces in her throat.

Then, as a reward, she would give her a piece of sausage.

As soon as she saw the man, Semillante would begin to tremble. Then she would look up to her mistress, who, lifting her finger, would cry, "Go!" in a shrill tone.

When she thought that the proper time had come, the widow went to confession and, one Sunday morning she partook of communion with an ecstatic fervor. Then, putting on men's clothes and looking like an old tramp, she struck a bargain with a Sardinian fisherman who carried her and her dog to the other side of the straits.

In a bag she had a large piece of sausage. Semillante had had nothing to eat for two days. The old woman kept letting her smell the food and whetting her appetite.

They got to Longosardo. The Corsican woman walked with a limp. She went to a baker's shop and asked for Nicolas Ravolati. He had taken up his old trade, that of carpenter. He was working alone at the back of his store.

The old woman opened the door and called:

"Hallo, Nicolas!"

He turned around. Then releasing her dog, she cried:

"Go, go! Eat him up! eat him up!"

The maddened animal sprang for his throat. The man stretched out his arms, clasped the dog and rolled to the ground. For a few seconds he squirmed, beating the ground with his feet. Then he stopped moving, while Semillante dug her fangs into his throat and tore it to ribbons. Two neighbors, seated before their door, remembered perfectly having seen an old beggar come out with a thin, black dog which was eating something that its master was giving him.

At nightfall the old woman was at home again. She slept well that night.

Father Milon

For a month the hot sun has been parching the fields. Nature is expanding beneath its rays; the fields are green as far as the eye can see. The big azure dome of the sky is unclouded. The farms of Normandy, scattered over the plains and surrounded by a belt of tall beeches, look, from a distance, like little woods. On closer view, after lowering the worm-eaten wooden bars, you imagine yourself in an immense garden, for all the ancient apple-trees, as gnarled as the peasants themselves, are in bloom. The sweet scent of their blossoms mingles with the heavy smell of the earth and the penetrating odor of the stables. It is noon. The family is eating under the shade of a pear tree planted in front of the door; father, mother, the four children, and the help—two women and three men are all there. All are silent. The soup is eaten and then a dish of potatoes fried with bacon is brought on.

From time to time one of the women gets up and takes a pitcher down to the cellar to fetch more cider.

The man, a big fellow about forty years old, is watching a grape vine, still bare, which is winding and twisting like a snake along the side of the house.

At last he says: "Father's vine is budding early this year. Perhaps we may get something from it."

The woman then turns round and looks, without saying a word.

This vine is planted on the spot where their father had

been shot.

It was during the war of 1870. The Prussians were occupying the whole country. General Faidherbe, with the Northern Division of the army, was opposing them.

The Prussians had established their headquarters at this farm. The old farmer to whom it belonged, Father Pierre Milon, had received and quartered them to the best of his ability.

For a month the German vanguard had been in this village. The French remained motionless, ten leagues away; and yet, every night, some of the Uhlans disappeared.

Of all the isolated scouts, of all those who were sent to the outposts, in groups of not more than three, not one ever returned.

They were picked up the next morning in a field or in a ditch. Even their horses were found along the roads with their throats cut.

These murders seemed to be done by the same men, who could never be found.

The country was terrorized. Farmers were shot on suspicion, women were imprisoned; children were frightened in order to try and obtain information. Nothing could be ascertained.

But, one morning, Father Milon was found stretched out in the barn, with a sword gash across his face.

Two Uhlans were found dead about a mile and a half from the farm. One of them was still holding his bloody sword in his hand. He had fought, tried to defend himself. A

15

court-martial was immediately held in the open air, in front of the farm. The old man was brought before it.

He was sixty-eight years old, small, thin, bent, with two big hands resembling the claws of a crab. His colorless hair was sparse and thin, like the down of a young duck, allowing patches of his scalp to be seen. The brown and wrinkled skin of his neck showed big veins which disappeared behind his jaws and came out again at the temples. He had the reputation of being miserly and hard to deal with.

They stood him up between four soldiers, in front of the kitchen table, which had been dragged outside. Five officers and the colonel seated themselves opposite him.

The colonel spoke in French:

"Father Milon, since we have been here we have only had praise for you. You have always been obliging and even attentive to us. But to-day a terrible accusation is hanging over you, and you must clear the matter up. How did you receive that wound on your face?"

The peasant answered nothing.

The colonel continued:

"Your silence accuses you, Father Milon. But I want you to answer me! Do you understand? Do you know who killed the two Uhlans who were found this morning near Calvaire?"

The old man answered clearly

"I did."

The colonel, surprised, was silent for a minute, looking straight at the prisoner. Father Milon stood impassive, with the stupid look of the peasant, his eyes lowered as though he were talking to the priest. Just one thing betrayed an uneasy mind; he was continually swallowing his saliva, with a visible effort, as though his throat were terribly contracted.

The man's family, his son Jean, his daughter-in-law and his two grandchildren were standing a few feet behind him, bewildered and affrighted.

The colonel went on:

"Do you also know who killed all the scouts who have been found dead, for a month, throughout the country, every morning?"

The old man answered with the same stupid look:

"I did."

"You killed them all?"

"Uh huh! I did."

"You alone? All alone?"

"Uh huh!"

"Tell me how you did it."

This time the man seemed moved; the necessity for talking any length of time annoyed him visibly. He stammered:

"I dunno! I simply did it."

The colonel continued:

"I warn you that you will have to tell me everything. You might as well make up your mind right away. How did you begin?"

The man cast a troubled look toward his family, standing close behind him. He hesitated a minute longer, and then suddenly made up his mind to obey the order.

"I was coming home one night at about ten o'clock, the

night after you got here. You and your soldiers had taken more than fifty ecus worth of forage from me, as well as a cow and two sheep. I said to myself: 'As much as they take from you; just so much will you make them pay back.' And then I had other things on my mind which I will tell you. Just then I noticed one of your soldiers who was smoking his pipe by the ditch behind the barn. I went and got my scythe and crept up slowly behind him, so that he couldn't hear me. And I cut his head off with one single blow, just as I would a blade of grass, before he could say 'Booh!' If you should look at the bottom of the pond, you will find him tied up in a potato-sack, with a stone fastened to it.

"I got an idea. I took all his clothes, from his boots to his cap, and hid them away in the little wood behind the yard."

The old man stopped. The officers remained speechless, looking at each other. The questioning began again, and this is what they learned.

Once this murder committed, the man had lived with this one thought: "Kill the Prussians!" He hated them with the blind, fierce hate of the greedy yet patriotic peasant. He had his idea, as he said. He waited several days.

He was allowed to go and come as he pleased, because he had shown himself so humble, submissive and obliging to the invaders. Each night he saw the outposts leave. One night he followed them, having heard the name of the village to which the men were going, and having learned the few words of German which he needed for his plan through associating with the soldiers.

He left through the back yard, slipped into the woods, found the dead man's clothes and put them on. Then he began to crawl through the fields, following along the hedges in order to keep out of sight, listening to the slightest noises, as wary as a poacher.

As soon as he thought the time ripe, he approached the road and hid behind a bush. He waited for a while. Finally, toward midnight, he heard the sound of a galloping horse. The man put his ear to the ground in order to make sure that only one horseman was approaching, then he got ready.

An Uhlan came galloping along, carrying des patches. As he went, he was all eyes and ears. When he was only a few feet away, Father Milon dragged himself across the road, moaning: "Hilfe! Hilfe!" (Help! Help!) The horseman stopped, and recognizing a German, he thought he was wounded and dismounted, coming nearer without any suspicion, and just as he was leaning over the unknown man, he received, in the pit of his stomach, a heavy thrust from the long curved blade of the sabre. He dropped without suffering pain, quivering only in the final throes. Then the farmer, radiant with the silent joy of an old peasant, got up again, and, for his own pleasure, cut the dead man's throat. He then dragged the body to the ditch and threw it in.

The horse quietly awaited its master. Father Milon mounted him and started galloping across the plains.

About an hour later he noticed two more Uhlans who were returning home, side by side. He rode straight for them, once more crying "Hilfe! Hilfe!"

The Prussians, recognizing the uniform, let him approach without distrust. The old man passed between them like a cannon-ball, felling them both, one with his sabre and the other with a revolver.

Then he killed the horses, German horses! After that he quickly returned to the woods and hid one of the horses. He left his uniform there and again put on his old clothes; then going back into bed, he slept until morning.

For four days he did not go out, waiting for the inquest to be terminated; but on the fifth day he went out again and killed two more soldiers by the same stratagem. From that time on he did not stop. Each night he wandered about in search of adventure, killing Prussians, sometimes here and sometimes there, galloping through deserted fields, in the moonlight, a lost Uhlan, a hunter of men. Then, his task accomplished, leaving behind him the bodies lying along the roads, the old farmer would return and hide his horse and uniform.

He went, toward noon, to carry oats and water quietly to his mount, and he fed it well as he required from it a great amount of work.

But one of those whom he had attacked the night before, in defending himself slashed the old peasant across the face with his sabre.

However, he had killed them both. He had come back and hidden the horse and put on his ordinary clothes again; but as he reached home he began to feel faint, and had dragged himself as far as the stable, being unable to reach the house.

They had found him there, bleeding, on the straw.

When he had finished his tale, he suddenly lifted up his head and looked proudly at the Prussian officers.

The colonel, who was gnawing at his mustache, asked:

"You have nothing else to say?"

"Nothing more; I have finished my task; I killed sixteen, not one more or less."

"Do you know that you are going to die?"

"I haven't asked for mercy."

"Have you been a soldier?"

"Yes, I served my time. And then, you had killed my father, who was a soldier of the first Emperor. And last month you killed my youngest son, Francois, near Evreux. I owed you one for that; I paid. We are quits."

The officers were looking at each other.

The old man continued:

"Eight for my father, eight for the boy—we are quits. I did not seek any quarrel with you. I don't know you. I don't even know where you come from. And here you are, ordering me about in my home as though it were your own. I took my revenge upon the others. I'm not sorry."

And, straightening up his bent back, the old man folded his arms in the attitude of a modest hero.

The Prussians talked in a low tone for a long time. One of them, a captain, who had also lost his son the previous month, was defending the poor wretch. Then the colonel arose and, approaching Father Milon, said in a low voice:

"Listen, old man, there is perhaps a way of saving your

life, it is to—"

But the man was not listening, and, his eyes fixed on the hated officer, while the wind played with the downy hair on his head, he distorted his slashed face, giving it a truly terrible expression, and, swelling out his chest, he spat, as hard as he could, right in the Prussian's face.

The colonel, furious, raised his hand, and for the second time the man spat in his face.

All the officers had jumped up and were shrieking orders at the same time.

In less than a minute the old man, still impassive, was pushed up against the wall and shot, looking smilingly the while toward Jean, his eldest son, his daughter-in-law and his two grandchildren, who witnessed this scene in dumb terror.

Mother Sauvage

Fifteen years had passed since I was at Virelogne. I returned there in the autumn to shoot with my friend Serval, who had at last rebuilt his chateau, which the Prussians had destroyed.

I loved that district. It is one of those delightful spots which have a sensuous charm for the eyes. You love it with a physical love. We, whom the country enchants, keep tender memories of certain springs, certain woods, certain pools, certain hills seen very often which have stirred us like joyful events. Sometimes our thoughts turn back to a corner in a forest, or the end of a bank, or an orchard filled with flowers, seen but a single time on some bright day, yet remaining in our hearts like the image of certain women met in the street on a spring morning in their light, gauzy dresses, leaving in soul and body an unsatisfied desire which is not to be forgotten, a feeling that you have just passed by happiness.

At Virelogne I loved the whole countryside, dotted with little woods and crossed by brooks which sparkled in the sun and looked like veins carrying blood to the earth. You fished in them for crawfish, trout and eels. Divine happiness! You could bathe in places and you often found snipe among the high grass which grew along the borders of these small water courses.

I was stepping along light as a goat, watching my two dogs running ahead of me, Serval, a hundred metres to my right, was beating a field of lucerne. I turned round by the thicket which forms the boundary of the wood of Sandres and I saw a cottage in ruins.

Suddenly I remembered it as I had seen it the last time, in 1869, neat, covered with vines, with chickens before the door. What is sadder than a dead house, with its skeleton standing bare and sinister?

I also recalled that inside its doors, after a very tiring day, the good woman had given me a glass of wine to drink and that Serval had told me the history of its people. The father, an old poacher, had been killed by the gendarmes. The son, whom I had once seen, was a tall, dry fellow who also passed for a fierce slayer of game. People called them "Les Sauvage."

Was that a name or a nickname?

I called to Serval. He came up with his long strides like a crane.

I asked him:

"What's become of those people?"

This was his story:

When war was declared the son Sauvage, who was then thirty-three years old, enlisted, leaving his mother alone in the house. People did not pity the old woman very much because she had money; they knew it.

She remained entirely alone in that isolated dwelling, so far from the village, on the edge of the wood. She was not afraid, however, being of the same strain as the men folk—a hardy old woman, tall and thin, who seldom laughed and with whom one never jested. The women of the fields laugh but little in any case, that is men's business. But they themselves have sad and narrowed hearts, leading a melancholy, gloomy life. The peasants imbibe a little noisy merriment at the tavern, but their helpmates always have grave, stern countenances. The muscles of their faces have never learned the motions of laughter.

Mother Sauvage continued her ordinary existence in her cottage, which was soon covered by the snows. She came to the village once a week to get bread and a little meat. Then she returned to her house. As there was talk of wolves, she went out with a gun upon her shoulder—her son's gun, rusty and with the butt worn by the rubbing of the hand—and she was a strange sight, the tall "Sauvage," a little bent, going with slow strides over the snow, the muzzle of the piece extending beyond the black headdress, which confined her head and imprisoned her white hair, which no one had ever seen.

One day a Prussian force arrived. It was billeted upon the inhabitants, according to the property and resources of each. Four were allotted to the old woman, who was known to be rich.

They were four great fellows with fair complexion, blond beards and blue eyes, who had not grown thin in spite of the fatigue which they had endured already and who also, though in a conquered country, had remained kind and gentle. Alone with this aged woman, they showed themselves full of consideration, sparing her, as much as they could, all expense and fatigue. They could be seen, all four of them, making their toilet at the well in their shirt-sleeves in the gray dawn, splashing with great swishes of water their pink-white northern skin, while La Mere Sauvage went and came, preparing their soup. They would be seen cleaning the kitchen, rubbing the tiles, splitting wood, peeling potatoes, doing up all the housework like four good sons around their mother.

But the old woman thought always of her own son, so tall and thin, with his hooked nose and his brown eyes and his heavy mustache which made a roll of black hair upon his lip. She asked every day of each of the soldiers who were installed beside her hearth: "Do you know where the French marching regiment, No. 23, was sent? My boy is in it."

They invariably answered, "No, we don't know, don't know a thing at all." And, understanding her pain and her uneasiness—they who had mothers, too, there at home—they rendered her a thousand little services. She loved them well, moreover, her four enemies, since the peasantry have no patriotic hatred; that belongs to the upper class alone. The humble, those who pay the most because they are poor and because every new burden crushes them down; those who are killed in masses, who make the true cannon's prey because they are so many; those, in fine, who suffer most cruelly the atrocious miseries of war because they are the feeblest and offer least resistance—they hardly understand at all those bellicose ardors, that excitable sense of honor or those pretended political combinations which in six months exhaust two nations, the conqueror with the conquered.

They said in the district, in speaking of the Germans of La Mere Sauvage:

"There are four who have found a soft place."

Now, one morning, when the old woman was alone in the house, she observed, far off on the plain, a man coming toward her dwelling. Soon she recognized him; it was the postman to distribute the letters. He gave her a folded paper and she drew out of her case the spectacles which she used for sewing. Then she read:

MADAME SAUVAGE: This letter is to tell you sad news. Your boy

Victor was killed yesterday by a shell which almost cut him in two.

I was near by, as we stood next each other in the company, and he

told me about you and asked me to let you know on the same day if

anything happened to him.

I took his watch, which was in his pocket, to bring it back to you

when the war is done.

CESAIRE RIVOT,

Soldier of the 2d class, March. Reg. No. 23.

The letter was dated three weeks back.

She did not cry at all. She remained motionless, so overcome and stupefied that she did not even suffer as yet. She thought: "There's Victor killed now." Then little by little the tears came to her eyes and the sorrow filled her heart. Her thoughts came, one by one, dreadful, torturing. She would never kiss him again, her child, her big boy, never again! The gendarmes had killed the father, the Prussians had killed the son. He had been cut in two by a cannon-ball. She seemed to see the thing, the horrible thing: the head falling, the eyes open, while he chewed the corner of his big mustache as he always did in moments of anger.

What had they done with his body afterward? If they had only let her have her boy back as they had brought back her husband—with the bullet in the middle of the forehead!

But she heard a noise of voices. It was the Prussians returning from the village. She hid her letter very quickly in her pocket, and she received them quietly, with her ordinary face, having had time to wipe her eyes.

They were laughing, all four, delighted, for they brought with them a fine rabbit—stolen, doubtless—and they made signs to the old woman that there was to be something good to east.

She set herself to work at once to prepare breakfast, but when it came to killing the rabbit, her heart failed her. And yet it was not the first. One of the soldiers struck it down with a blow of his fist behind the ears.

The beast once dead, she skinned the red body, but the sight of the blood which she was touching, and which covered her hands, and which she felt cooling and coagulating, made her tremble from head to foot, and she kept seeing her big boy cut in two, bloody, like this still palpitating animal.

She sat down at table with the Prussians, but she could

not eat, not even a mouthful. They devoured the rabbit without bothering themselves about her. She looked at them sideways, without speaking, her face so impassive that they perceived nothing.

All of a sudden she said: "I don't even know your names, and here's a whole month that we've been together." They understood, not without difficulty, what she wanted, and told their names.

That was not sufficient; she had them written for her on a paper, with the addresses of their families, and, resting her spectacles on her great nose, she contemplated that strange handwriting, then folded the sheet and put it in her pocket, on top of the letter which told her of the death of her son.

When the meal was ended she said to the men:

"I am going to work for you."

And she began to carry up hay into the loft where they slept.

They were astonished at her taking all this trouble; she explained to them that thus they would not be so cold; and they helped her. They heaped the stacks of hay as high as the straw roof, and in that manner they made a sort of great chamber with four walls of fodder, warm and perfumed, where they should sleep splendidly.

At dinner one of them was worried to see that La Mère Sauvage still ate nothing. She told him that she had pains in her stomach. Then she kindled a good fire to warm herself, and the four Germans ascended to their lodging-place by the ladder which served them every night for this purpose.

As soon as they closed the trapdoor the old woman removed the ladder, then opened the outside door noiselessly and went back to look for more bundles of straw, with which she filled her kitchen. She went barefoot in the snow, so softly that no sound was heard. From time to time she listened to the sonorous and unequal snoring of the four soldiers who were fast asleep.

When she judged her preparations to be sufficient, she threw one of the bundles into the fireplace, and when it was alight she scattered it over all the others. Then she went outside again and looked.

In a few seconds the whole interior of the cottage was illumined with a brilliant light and became a frightful brasier, a gigantic fiery furnace, whose glare streamed out of the narrow window and threw a glittering beam upon the snow.

Then a great cry issued from the top of the house; it was a clamor of men shouting heartrending calls of anguish and of terror. Finally the trapdoor having given way, a whirlwind of fire shot up into the loft, pierced the straw roof, rose to the sky like the immense flame of a torch, and all the cottage flared.

Nothing more was heard therein but the crackling of the fire, the cracking of the walls, the falling of the rafters. Suddenly the roof fell in and the burning carcass of the dwelling hurled a great plume of sparks into the air, amid a cloud of smoke.

The country, all white, lit up by the fire, shone like a cloth of silver tinted with red.

A bell, far off, began to toll.

The old "Sauvage" stood before her ruined dwelling, armed with her gun, her son's gun, for fear one of those men might escape.

When she saw that it was ended, she threw her weapon into the brasier. A loud report followed.

People were coming, the peasants, the Prussians.

They found the woman seated on the trunk of a tree, calm and satisfied.

A German officer, but speaking French like a son of France, demanded:

"Where are your soldiers?"

She reached her bony arm toward the red heap of fire which was almost out and answered with a strong voice:

"There!"

They crowded round her. The Prussian asked:

"How did it take fire?"

"It was I who set it on fire."

They did not believe her, they thought that the sudden disaster had made her crazy. While all pressed round and listened, she told the story from beginning to end, from the arrival of the letter to the last shriek of the men who were burned with her house, and never omitted a detail.

When she had finished, she drew two pieces of paper from her pocket, and, in order to distinguish them by the last gleams of the fire, she again adjusted her spectacles. Then she said, showing one:

"That, that is the death of Victor." Showing the other,

she added, indicating the red ruins with a bend of the head: "Here are their names, so that you can write home." She quietly held a sheet of paper out to the officer, who held her by the shoulders, and she continued:

"You must write how it happened, and you must say to their mothers that it was I who did that, Victoire Simon, la Sauvage! Do not forget."

The officer shouted some orders in German. They seized her, they threw her against the walls of her house, still hot. Then twelve men drew quickly up before her, at twenty paces. She did not move. She had understood; she waited.

An order rang out, followed instantly by a long report. A belated shot went off by itself, after the others.

The old woman did not fall. She sank as though they had cut off her legs.

The Prussian officer approached. She was almost cut in two, and in her withered hand she held her letter bathed with blood.

My friend Serval added:

"It was by way of reprisal that the Germans destroyed the chateau of the district, which belonged to me."

I thought of the mothers of those four fine fellows burned in that house and of the horrible heroism of that other mother shot against the wall.

And I picked up a little stone, still blackened by the flames.

The Corsican Bandit

The road ascended gently through the forest of Aitone. The large pines formed a solemn dome above our heads, and that mysterious sound made by the wind in the trees sounded like the notes of an organ.

After walking for three hours, there was a clearing, and then at intervals an enormous pine umbrella, and then we suddenly came to the edge of the forest, some hundred meters below, the pass leading to the wild valley of Niolo.

On the two projecting heights which commanded a view of this pass, some old trees, grotesquely twisted, seemed to have mounted with painful efforts, like scouts sent in advance of the multitude in the rear. When we turned round, we saw the entire forest stretched beneath our feet, like a gigantic basin of verdure, inclosed by bare rocks whose summits seemed to reach the sky.

We resumed our walk, and, ten minutes later, found ourselves in the pass.

Then I beheld a remarkable landscape. Beyond another forest stretched a valley, but a valley such as I had never seen before; a solitude of stone, ten leagues long, hollowed out between two high mountains, without a field or a tree to be seen. This was the Niolo valley, the fatherland of Corsican liberty, the inaccessible citadel, from which the invaders had never been able to drive out the mountaineers.

My companion said to me: "This is where all our bandits have taken refuge?"

Ere long we were at the further end of this gorge, so wild, so inconceivably beautiful.

Not a blade of grass, not a plant-nothing but granite. As far as our eyes could reach, we saw in front of us a desert of glittering stone, heated like an oven by a burning sun, which seemed to hang for that very purpose right above the gorge. When we raised our eyes towards the crests, we stood dazzled and stupefied by what we saw. They looked like a festoon of coral; all the summits are of porphyry; and the sky overhead was violet, purple, tinged with the coloring of these strange mountains. Lower down, the granite was of scintillating gray, and seemed ground to powder beneath our feet. At our right, along a long and irregular course, roared a tumultuous torrent. And we staggered along under this heat, in this light, in this burning, arid, desolate valley cut by this torrent of turbulent water which seemed to be ever hurrying onward, without fertilizing the rocks, lost in this furnace which greedily drank it up without being saturated or refreshed by it.

But, suddenly, there was visible at our right a little wooden cross sunk in a little heap of stones. A man had been killed there; and I said to my companion.

"Tell me about your bandits."

He replied:

"I knew the most celebrated of them, the terrible St. Lucia. I will tell you his history.

"His father was killed in a quarrel by a young man of the district, it is said; and St. Lucia was left alone with his sister. He was a weak, timid youth, small, often ill, without any energy. He did not proclaim vengeance against the assassin of his father. All his relatives came to see him, and implored of him to avenge his death; he remained deaf to their menaces and their supplications.

"Then, following the old Corsican custom, his sister, in her indignation carried away his black clothes, in order that he might not wear mourning for a dead man who had not been avenged. He was insensible to even this affront, and rather than take down from the rack his father's gun, which was still loaded, he shut himself up, not daring to brave the looks of the young men of the district.

"He seemed to have even forgotten the crime, and lived with his sister in the seclusion of their dwelling.

"But, one day, the man who was suspected of having committed the murder, was about to get married. St. Lucia did not appear to be moved by this news, but, out of sheer bravado, doubtless, the bridegroom, on his way to the church, passed before the house of the two orphans.

"The brother and the sister, at their window, were eating frijoles, when the young man saw the bridal procession going by. Suddenly he began to tremble, rose to his feet without uttering a word, made the sign of the cross, took the gun which was hanging over the fireplace, and went out.

"When he spoke of this later on, he said: 'I don't know what was the matter with me; it was like fire in my blood; I felt that I must do it, that, in spite of everything, I could not resist, and I concealed the gun in a cave on the road to Corte.

"An hour later, he came back, with nothing in his hand, and with his habitual air of sad weariness. His sister believed that there was nothing further in his thoughts.

"But when night fell he disappeared.

"His enemy had, the same evening, to repair to Corte on foot, accompanied by his two groomsmen.

"He was walking along, singing as he went, when St. Lucia stood before him, and looking straight in the murderer's face, exclaimed: 'Now is the time!' and shot him point-blank in the chest.

"One of the men fled; the other stared at, the young man, saying:

"'What have you done, St. Lucia?' and he was about to hasten to Corte for help, when St. Lucia said in a stern tone:

"'If you move another step, I'll shoot you in the leg.'

"The other, aware of his timidity hitherto, replied: 'You would not dare to do it!' and was hurrying off when he fell instantaneously, his thigh shattered by a bullet.

"And St. Lucia, coming over to where he lay, said:

"'I am going to look at your wound; if it is not serious, I'll leave you there; if it is mortal I'll finish you off."

"He inspected the wound, considered it mortal, and slowly reloading his gun, told the wounded man to say a prayer, and shot him through the head.

"Next day he was in the mountains.

"And do you know what this St. Lucia did after this?

"All his family were arrested by the gendarmes. His uncle, the cure, who was suspected of having incited him to this deed of vengeance, was himself put in prison, and accused by the dead man's relatives. But he escaped, took a gun in his turn, and went to join his nephew in the brush.

"Next, St. Lucia killed, one after the other, his uncle's accusers, and tore out their eyes to teach the others never to state what they had seen with their eyes.

"He killed all the relatives, all the connections of his enemy's family. He slew during his life fourteen gendarmes, burned down the houses of his adversaries, and was, up to the day of his death, the most terrible of all the bandits whose memory we have preserved."

The sun disappeared behind Monte Cinto and the tall shadow of the granite mountain went to sleep on the granite of the valley. We quickened our pace in order to reach before night the little village of Albertaccio, nothing but a pile of stones welded into the stone flanks of a wild gorge. And I said as I thought of the bandit:

"What a terrible custom your vendetta is!"

My companion answered with an air of resignation:

"What would you have? A man must do his duty!"

The Hand

All were crowding around M. Bermutier, the judge, who was giving his opinion about the Saint-Cloud mystery. For a month this in explicable crime had been the talk of Paris. Nobody could make head or tail of it.

M. Bermutier, standing with his back to the fireplace, was talking, citing the evidence, discussing the various theories, but arriving at no conclusion.

Some women had risen, in order to get nearer to him, and were standing with their eyes fastened on the clean-shaven face of the judge, who was saying such weighty things. They, were shaking and trembling, moved by fear and curiosity, and by the eager and insatiable desire for the horrible, which haunts the soul of every woman. One of them, paler than the others, said during a pause:

"It's terrible. It verges on the supernatural. The truth will never be known."

The judge turned to her:

"True, madame, it is likely that the actual facts will never be discovered. As for the word 'supernatural' which you have just used, it has nothing to do with the matter. We are in the presence of a very cleverly conceived and executed crime, so well enshrouded in mystery that we cannot disentangle it from the involved circumstances which surround it. But once I had to take charge of an affair in which the uncanny seemed to play a part. In fact, the case became so confused that it had to be given up."

Several women exclaimed at once:

"Oh! Tell us about it!"

M. Bermutier smiled in a dignified manner, as a judge should, and went on:

"Do not think, however, that I, for one minute, ascribed anything in the case to supernatural influences. I believe only in normal causes. But if, instead of using the word 'supernatural' to express what we do not understand, we were simply to make use of the word 'inexplicable,' it would be much better. At any rate, in the affair of which I am about to tell you, it is especially the surrounding, preliminary circumstances which impressed me. Here are the facts:

"I was, at that time, a judge at Ajaccio, a little white city on the edge of a bay which is surrounded by high mountains.

"The majority of the cases which came up before me concerned vendettas. There are some that are superb, dramatic, ferocious, heroic. We find there the most beautiful causes for revenge of which one could dream, enmities hundreds of years old, quieted for a time but never extinguished; abominable stratagems, murders becoming massacres and almost deeds of glory. For two years I heard of nothing but the price of blood, of this terrible Corsican prejudice which compels revenge for insults meted out to the offending person and all his descendants and relatives. I had seen old men, children, cousins murdered; my head was full of these stories.

"One day I learned that an Englishman had just hired a little villa at the end of the bay for several years. He had brought with him a French servant, whom he had engaged on the way at Marseilles.

"Soon this peculiar person, living alone, only going out to hunt and fish, aroused a widespread interest. He never spoke to any one, never went to the town, and every morning he would practice for an hour or so with his revolver and rifle.

"Legends were built up around him. It was said that he was some high personage, fleeing from his fatherland for political reasons; then it was affirmed that he was in hiding after having committed some abominable crime. Some particularly horrible circumstances were even mentioned.

"In my judicial position I thought it necessary to get some information about this man, but it was impossible to learn anything. He called himself Sir John Rowell.

"I therefore had to be satisfied with watching him as closely as I could, but I could see nothing suspicious about his actions.

"However, as rumors about him were growing and becoming more widespread, I decided to try to see this stranger myself, and I began to hunt regularly in the neighborhood of his grounds.

"For a long time I watched without finding an opportunity. At last it came to me in the shape of a partridge which I shot and killed right in front of the Englishman. My dog fetched it for me, but, taking the bird, I went at once to Sir John Rowell and, begging his pardon, asked him to accept it.

"He was a big man, with red hair and beard, very tall, very broad, a kind of calm and polite Hercules. He had nothing of the so-called British stiffness, and in a broad English accent he thanked me warmly for my attention. At the end of a month we had had five or six conversations.

"One night, at last, as I was passing before his door, I saw him in the garden, seated astride a chair, smoking his pipe. I bowed and he invited me to come in and have a glass of beer. I needed no urging.

"He received me with the most punctilious English courtesy, sang the praises of France and of Corsica, and declared that he was quite in love with this country.

"Then, with great caution and under the guise of a vivid interest, I asked him a few questions about his life and his plans. He answered without embarrassment, telling me that he had travelled a great deal in Africa, in the Indies, in America. He added, laughing:

"'I have had many adventures.'

"Then I turned the conversation on hunting, and he gave me the most curious details on hunting the hippopotamus, the tiger, the elephant and even the gorilla.

"I said:

"'Are all these animals dangerous?'

"He smiled:

"'Oh, no! Man is the worst.'

"And he laughed a good broad laugh, the wholesome laugh of a contented Englishman.

"'I have also frequently been man-hunting.'

"Then he began to talk about weapons, and he invited me to come in and see different makes of guns.

"His parlor was draped in black, black silk embroidered

in gold. Big yellow flowers, as brilliant as fire, were worked on the dark material.

"He said:

"'It is a Japanese material.'

"But in the middle of the widest panel a strange thing attracted my attention. A black object stood out against a square of red velvet. I went up to it; it was a hand, a human hand. Not the clean white hand of a skeleton, but a dried black hand, with yellow nails, the muscles exposed and traces of old blood on the bones, which were cut off as clean as though it had been chopped off with an axe, near the middle of the forearm.

"Around the wrist, an enormous iron chain, riveted and soldered to this unclean member, fastened it to the wall by a ring, strong enough to hold an elephant in leash.

"I asked:

"'What is that?'

"The Englishman answered quietly:

"'That is my best enemy. It comes from America, too. The bones were severed by a sword and the skin cut off with a sharp stone and dried in the sun for a week.'

"I touched these human remains, which must have belonged to a giant. The uncommonly long fingers were attached by enormous tendons which still had pieces of skin hanging to them in places. This hand was terrible to see; it made one think of some savage vengeance.

"I said:

"'This man must have been very strong.'

42

"The Englishman answered quietly:

"'Yes, but I was stronger than he. I put on this chain to hold him.'

"I thought that he was joking. I said:

"'This chain is useless now, the hand won't run away.'

"Sir John Rowell answered seriously:

"'It always wants to go away. This chain is needed.'

"I glanced at him quickly, questioning his face, and I asked myself:

"'Is he an insane man or a practical joker?'

"But his face remained inscrutable, calm and friendly. I turned to other subjects, and admired his rifles.

"However, I noticed that he kept three loaded revolvers in the room, as though constantly in fear of some attack.

"I paid him several calls. Then I did not go any more. People had become used to his presence; everybody had lost interest in him.

"A whole year rolled by. One morning, toward the end of November, my servant awoke me and announced that Sir John Rowell had been murdered during the night.

"Half an hour later I entered the Englishman's house, together with the police commissioner and the captain of the gendarmes. The servant, bewildered and in despair, was crying before the door. At first I suspected this man, but he was innocent.

"The guilty party could never be found.

"On entering Sir John's parlor, I noticed the body, stretched out on its back, in the middle of the room.

43

"His vest was torn, the sleeve of his jacket had been pulled off, everything pointed to, a violent struggle.

"The Englishman had been strangled! His face was black, swollen and frightful, and seemed to express a terrible fear. He held something between his teeth, and his neck, pierced by five or six holes which looked as though they had been made by some iron instrument, was covered with blood.

"A physician joined us. He examined the finger marks on the neck for a long time and then made this strange announcement:

"'It looks as though he had been strangled by a skeleton.'

"A cold chill seemed to run down my back, and I looked over to where I had formerly seen the terrible hand. It was no longer there. The chain was hanging down, broken.

"I bent over the dead man and, in his contracted mouth, I found one of the fingers of this vanished hand, cut—or rather sawed off by the teeth down to the second knuckle.

"Then the investigation began. Nothing could be discovered. No door, window or piece of furniture had been forced. The two watch dogs had not been aroused from their sleep.

"Here, in a few words, is the testimony of the servant:

"For a month his master had seemed excited. He had received many letters, which he would immediately burn.

"Often, in a fit of passion which approached madness, he had taken a switch and struck wildly at this dried hand riveted to the wall, and which had disappeared, no one knows how, at the very hour of the crime.

"He would go to bed very late and carefully lock himself in. He always kept weapons within reach. Often at night he would talk loudly, as though he were quarrelling with some one.

"That night, somehow, he had made no noise, and it was only on going to open the windows that the servant had found Sir John murdered. He suspected no one.

"I communicated what I knew of the dead man to the judges and public officials. Throughout the whole island a minute investigation was carried on. Nothing could be found out.

"One night, about three months after the crime, I had a terrible nightmare. I seemed to see the horrible hand running over my curtains and walls like an immense scorpion or spider. Three times I awoke, three times I went to sleep again; three times I saw the hideous object galloping round my room and moving its fingers like legs.

"The following day the hand was brought me, found in the cemetery, on the grave of Sir John Rowell, who had been buried there because we had been unable to find his family. The first finger was missing.

"Ladies, there is my story. I know nothing more."

The women, deeply stirred, were pale and trembling. One of them exclaimed:

"But that is neither a climax nor an explanation! We will be unable to sleep unless you give us your opinion of what had occurred."

The judge smiled severely:

"Oh! Ladies, I shall certainly spoil your terrible dreams. I simply believe that the legitimate owner of the hand was not dead, that he came to get it with his remaining one. But I don't know how. It was a kind of vendetta."

One of the women murmured:

"No, it can't be that."

And the judge, still smiling, said:

"Didn't I tell you that my explanation would not satisfy you?"

The Lancer's Wife

I

It was after Bourbaki's defeat in the east of France. The army, broken up, decimated, and worn out, had been obliged to retreat into Switzerland after that terrible campaign, and it was only its short duration that saved a hundred and fifty thousand men from certain death. Hunger, the terrible cold, forced marches in the snow without boots, over bad mountain roads, had caused us 'francs-tireurs', especially, the greatest suffering, for we were without tents, and almost without food, always in the van when we were marching toward Belfort, and in the rear when returning by the Jura. Of our little band that had numbered twelve hundred men on the first of January, there remained only twenty-two pale, thin, ragged wretches, when we at length succeeded in reaching Swiss territory.

There we were safe, and could rest. Everybody knows what sympathy was shown to the unfortunate French army, and how well it was cared for. We all gained fresh life, and those who had been rich and happy before the war declared that they had never experienced a greater feeling of comfort than they did then. Just think. We actually had something to eat every day, and could sleep every night.

Meanwhile, the war continued in the east of France, which had been excluded from the armistice. Besancon still kept the enemy in check, and the latter had their revenge by ravaging Franche Comte. Sometimes we heard that they had approached quite close to the frontier, and we saw Swiss troops, who were to form a line of observation between us and them, set out on their march.

That pained us in the end, and, as we regained health and strength, the longing to fight took possession of us. It was disgraceful and irritating to know that within two or three leagues of us the Germans were victorious and insolent, to feel that we were protected by our captivity, and to feel that on that account we were powerless against them.

One day our captain took five or six of us aside, and spoke to us about it, long and furiously. He was a fine fellow, that captain. He had been a sublieutenant in the Zouaves, was tall and thin and as hard as steel, and during the whole campaign he had cut out their work for the Germans. He fretted in inactivity, and could not accustom himself to the idea of being a prisoner and of doing nothing.

"Confound it!" he said to us, "does it not pain you to know that there is a number of uhlans within two hours of us? Does it not almost drive you mad to know that those beggarly wretches are walking about as masters in our mountains, when six determined men might kill a whole spitful any day? I cannot endure it any longer, and I must go there."

"But how can you manage it, captain?"

"How? It is not very difficult! Just as if we had not done a thing or two within the last six months, and got out of woods that were guarded by very different men from the Swiss. The day that you wish to cross over into France, I will undertake to get you there."

"That may be; but what shall we do in France without any arms?"

"Without arms? We will get them over yonder, by Jove!"

"You are forgetting the treaty," another soldier said; "we shall run the risk of doing the Swiss an injury, if Manteuffel learns that they have allowed prisoners to return to France."

"Come," said the captain, "those are all bad reasons. I mean to go and kill some Prussians; that is all I care about. If you do not wish to do as I do, well and good; only say so at once. I can quite well go by myself; I do not require anybody's company."

Naturally we all protested, and, as it was quite impossible to make the captain alter his mind, we felt obliged to promise to go with him. We liked him too much to leave him in the lurch, as he never failed us in any extremity; and so the expedition was decided on.

II

The captain had a plan of his own, that he had been cogitating over for some time. A man in that part of the country whom he knew was going to lend him a cart and six suits of peasants' clothes. We could hide under some straw at the bottom of the wagon, which would be loaded with Gruyere cheese, which he was supposed to be going to sell in France. The captain told the sentinels that he was taking two friends with him to protect his goods, in case any one should try to rob him, which did not seem an extraordinary precaution. A Swiss officer seemed to look at the wagon in a knowing manner, but that was in order to impress his soldiers. In a word, neither officers nor men could make it out.

"Get up," the captain said to the horses, as he cracked his whip, while our three men quietly smoked their pipes. I was half suffocated in my box, which only admitted the air through those holes in front, and at the same time I was nearly frozen, for it was terribly cold.

"Get up," the captain said again, and the wagon loaded with Gruyere cheese entered France.

The Prussian lines were very badly guarded, as the enemy trusted to the watchfulness of the Swiss. The sergeant spoke North German, while our captain spoke the bad German of the Four Cantons, and so they could not understand each other. The sergeant, however, pretended to be very intelligent; and, in order to make us believe that he understood us, they allowed us to continue our journey; and, after travelling for seven hours, being continually stopped in the same manner, we arrived at a small village of the Jura in ruins, at nightfall.

What were we going to do? Our only arms were the captain's whip, our uniforms our peasants' blouses, and our food the Gruyere cheese. Our sole wealth consisted in our ammunition, packages of cartridges which we had stowed away inside some of the large cheeses. We had about a thousand of them, just two hundred each, but we needed rifles, and they must be chassepots. Luckily, however, the captain was a bold man of an inventive mind, and this was the plan that he hit upon:

While three of us remained hidden in a cellar in the abandoned village, he continued his journey as far as Besancon with the empty wagon and one man. The town was invested, but one can always make one's way into a town among the hills by crossing the tableland till within about ten miles of the walls, and then following paths and ravines on foot. They left their wagon at Omans, among the Germans, and escaped out of it at night on foot; so as to gain the heights which border the River Doubs; the next day they entered Besancon, where there were plenty of chassepots. There were nearly forty thousand of them left in the arsenal, and General Roland, a brave marine, laughed at the captain's daring project, but let him have six rifles and wished him "good luck." There he had also found his wife, who had been through all the war with us before the campaign in the East, and who had been only prevented by illness from continuing

51

with Bourbaki's army. She had recovered, however, in spite of the cold, which was growing more and more intense, and in spite of the numberless privations that awaited her, she persisted in accompanying her husband. He was obliged to give way to her, and they all three, the captain, his wife, and our comrade, started on their expedition.

Going was nothing in comparison to returning. They were obliged to travel by night, so as to avoid meeting anybody, as the possession of six rifles would have made them liable to suspicion. But, in spite of everything, a week after leaving us, the captain and his two men were back with us again. The campaign was about to begin.

III

The first night of his arrival he began it himself, and, under pretext of examining the surrounding country, he went along the high road.

I must tell you that the little village which served as our fortress was a small collection of poor, badly built houses, which had been deserted long before. It lay on a steep slope, which terminated in a wooded plain. The country people sell the wood; they send it down the slopes, which are called coulees, locally, and which lead down to the plain, and there they stack it into piles, which they sell thrice a year to the wood merchants. The spot where this market is held in indicated by two small houses by the side of the highroad, which serve for public houses. The captain had gone down there by way of one of these coulees.

He had been gone about half an hour, and we were on the lookout at the top of the ravine, when we heard a shot. The captain had ordered us not to stir, and only to come to him when we heard him blow his trumpet. It was made of a goat's horn, and could be heard a league off; but it gave no sound, and, in spite of our cruel anxiety, we were obliged to wait in silence, with our rifles by our side.

It is nothing to go down these coulees; one just lets one's self slide down; but it is more difficult to get up again; one has to scramble up by catching hold of the hanging branches of the trees, and sometimes on all fours, by sheer strength. A whole mortal hour passed, and he did not come; nothing moved in the brushwood. The captain's wife began to grow impatient. What could he be doing? Why did he not call us? Did the shot that we had heard proceed from an enemy, and had he killed or wounded our leader, her husband? They did not know what to think, but I myself fancied either that he was dead or that his enterprise was successful; and I was merely anxious and curious to know what he had done.

Suddenly we heard the sound of his trumpet, and we were much surprised that instead of coming from below, as we had expected, it came from the village behind us. What did that mean? It was a mystery to us, but the same idea struck us all, that he had been killed, and that the Prussians were blowing the trumpet to draw us into an ambush. We therefore returned to the cottage, keeping a careful lookout with our fingers on the trigger, and hiding under the branches; but his wife, in spite of our entreaties, rushed on, leaping like a tigress. She thought that she had to avenge her husband, and had fixed the bayonet to her rifle, and we lost sight of her at the moment that we heard the trumpet again; and, a few moments later, we heard her calling out to us:

"Come on! come on! He is alive! It is he!"

We hastened on, and saw the captain smoking his pipe at the entrance of the village, but strangely enough, he was on horseback.

"Ah! ah!" he said to us, "you see that there is something to be done here. Here I am on horseback already; I knocked over an uhlan yonder, and took his horse; I suppose they were guarding the wood, but it was by drinking and swilling in clover. One of them, the sentry at the door, had not time to see me before I gave him a sugarplum in his stomach, and then, before the others could come out, I jumped on the horse and was off like a shot. Eight or ten of them followed me, I think; but I took the crossroads through the woods. I have got scratched and torn a bit, but here I am, and now, my good fellows, attention, and take care! Those brigands will not rest until they have caught us, and we must receive them with rifle bullets. Come along; let us take up our posts!"

We set out. One of us took up his position a good way from the village on the crossroads; I was posted at the entrance of the main street, where the road from the level country enters the village, while the two others, the captain and his wife, were in the middle of the village, near the church, whose tower-served for an observatory and citadel.

We had not been in our places long before we heard a shot, followed by another, and then two, then three. The first was evidently a chassepot —one recognized it by the sharp report, which sounds like the crack of a whip—while the other three came from the lancers' carbines.

The captain was furious. He had given orders to the outpost to let the enemy pass and merely to follow them at a distance if they marched toward the village, and to join me when they had gone well between the houses. Then they were to appear suddenly, take the patrol between two fires, and not allow a single man to escape; for, posted as we were, the six of us could have hemmed in ten Prussians, if needful.

"That confounded Piedelot has roused them," the captain

said, "and they will not venture to come on blindfolded any longer. And then I am quite sure that he has managed to get a shot into himself somewhere or other, for we hear nothing of him. It serves him right; why did he not obey orders?" And then, after a moment, he grumbled in his beard: "After all I am sorry for the poor fellow; he is so brave, and shoots so well!"

The captain was right in his conjectures. We waited until evening, without seeing the uhlans; they had retreated after the first attack; but unfortunately we had not seen Piedelot, either. Was he dead or a prisoner? When night came, the captain proposed that we should go out and look for him, and so the three of us started. At the crossroads we found a broken rifle and some blood, while the ground was trampled down; but we did not find either a wounded man or a dead body, although we searched every thicket, and at midnight we returned without having discovered anything of our unfortunate comrade.

"It is very strange," the captain growled. "They must have killed him and thrown him into the bushes somewhere; they cannot possibly have taken him prisoner, as he would have called out for help. I cannot understand it at all." Just as he said that, bright flames shot up in the direction of the inn on the high road, which illuminated the sky.

"Scoundrels! cowards!" he shouted. "I will bet that they have set fire to the two houses on the marketplace, in order to have their revenge, and then they will scuttle off without saying a word. They will be satisfied with having killed a man and set fire to two houses. All right. It shall not pass over like that. We must go for them; they will not like to leave their illuminations in order to fight."

"It would be a great stroke of luck if we could set Piedelot free at the same time," some one said.

The five of us set off, full of rage and hope. In twenty minutes we had got to the bottom of the coulee, and had not yet seen any one when we were within a hundred yards of the inn. The fire was behind the house, and all we saw of it was the reflection above the roof. However, we were walking rather slowly, as we were afraid of an ambush, when suddenly we heard Piedelot's well-known voice. It had a strange sound, however; for it was at the same time—dull and vibrating, stifled and clear, as if he were calling out as loud as he could with a bit of rag stuffed into his mouth. He seemed to be hoarse and gasping, and the unlucky fellow kept exclaiming: "Help! Help!"

We sent all thoughts of prudence to the devil, and in two bounds we were at the back of the inn, where a terrible sight met our eyes.

IV

Piedelot was being burned alive. He was writhing in the midst of a heap of fagots, tied to a stake, and the flames were licking him with their burning tongues. When he saw us, his tongue seemed to stick in his throat; he drooped his head, and seemed as if he were going to die. It was only the affair of a moment to upset the burning pile, to scatter the embers, and to cut the ropes that fastened him.

Poor fellow! In what a terrible state we found him. The evening before he had had his left arm broken, and it seemed as if he had been badly beaten since then, for his whole body was covered with wounds, bruises and blood. The flames had also begun their work on him, and he had two large burns, one on his loins and the other on his right thigh, and his beard and hair were scorched. Poor Piedelot!

No one knows the terrible rage we felt at this sight! We would have rushed headlong at a hundred thousand Prussians; our thirst for vengeance was intense. But the cowards had run away, leaving their crime behind them. Where could we find them now? Meanwhile, however, the captain's wife was looking after Piedelot, and dressing his wounds as best she could, while the captain himself shook hands with him excitedly, and in a few minutes he came to himself.

"Good-morning, captain; good-morning, all of you," he said. "Ah! the scoundrels, the wretches! Why, twenty of them came to surprise us."

"Twenty, do you say?"

"Yes; there was a whole band of them, and that is why I disobeyed orders, captain, and fired on them, for they would have killed you all, and I preferred to stop them. That frightened them, and they did not venture to go farther than the crossroads. They were such cowards. Four of them shot at me at twenty yards, as if I had been a target, and then they slashed me with their swords. My arm was broken, so that I could only use my bayonet with one hand."

"But why did you not call for help?"

"I took good care not to do that, for you would all have come; and you would neither have been able to defend me nor yourselves, being only five against twenty."

"You know that we should not have allowed you to have been taken, poor old fellow."

"I preferred to die by myself, don't you see! I did not want to bring you here, for it would have been a mere ambush."

"Well, we will not talk about it any more. Do you feel rather easier?"

"No, I am suffocating. I know that I cannot live much longer. The brutes! They tied me to a tree, and beat me till I was half dead, and then they shook my broken arm; but I did not make a sound. I would rather have bitten my tongue out than have called out before them. Now I can tell what I am suffering and shed tears; it does one good. Thank you, my kind friends."

"Poor Piedelot! But we will avenge you, you may be sure!"

"Yes, yes; I want you to do that. There is, in particular, a woman among them who passes as the wife of the lancer whom the captain killed yesterday. She is dressed like a lancer, and she tortured me the most yesterday, and suggested burning me; and it was she who set fire to the wood. Oh! the wretch, the brute! Ah! how I am suffering! My loins, my arms!" and he fell back gasping and exhausted, writhing in his terrible agony, while the captain's wife wiped the perspiration from his forehead, and we all shed tears of grief and rage, as if we had been children. I will not describe the end to you; he died half an hour later, previously telling us in what direction the enemy had gone. When he was dead we gave ourselves time to bury him, and then we set out in pursuit of them, with our hearts full of fury and hatred.

"We will throw ourselves on the whole Prussian army, if it be necessary," the captain said; "but we will avenge Piedelot. We must catch those scoundrels. Let us swear to die, rather than not to find them; and if I am killed first, these are my orders: All the prisoners that you take are to be shot immediately, and as for the lancer's wife, she is to be tortured before she is put to death."

"She must not be shot, because she is a woman," the captain's wife said. "If you survive, I am sure that you would not shoot a woman. Torturing her will be quite sufficient; but if you are killed in this pursuit, I want one thing, and that is to fight with her; I will kill her with my own hands, and the others can do what they like with her if she kills me."

"We will outrage her! We will burn her! We will tear her to pieces! Piedelot shall be avenged!

"An eye for an eye, a tooth for a tooth!"

V

The next morning we unexpectedly fell on an outpost of uhlans four leagues away. Surprised by our sudden attack, they were not able to mount their horses, nor even to defend themselves; and in a few moments we had five prisoner, corresponding to our own number. The captain questioned them, and from their answers we felt certain that they were the same whom we had encountered the previous day. Then a very curious operation took place. One of us was told off to ascertain their sex, and nothing can describe our joy when we discovered what we were seeking among them, the female executioner who had tortured our friend.

The four others were shot on the spot, with their backs to us and close to the muzzles of our rifles; and then we turned our attention to the woman. What were we going to do with her? I must acknowledge that we were all of us in favor of shooting her. Hatred, and the wish to avenge Piedelot, had extinguished all pity in us, and we had forgotten that we were going to shoot a woman, but a woman reminded us of it, the captain's wife; at her entreaties, therefore, we determined to keep her a prisoner.

The captain's poor wife was to be severely punished for this act of clemency.

The next day we heard that the armistice had been extended to the eastern part of France, and we had to put an end to our little campaign. Two of us, who belonged to the neighborhood, returned home, so there were only four of us, all told: the captain, his wife, and two men. We belonged to Besancon, which was still being besieged in spite of the armistice.

"Let us stop here," said the captain. "I cannot believe that the war is going to end like this. The devil take it! Surely there are men still left in France; and now is the time to prove what they are made of. The spring is coming on, and the armistice is only a trap laid for the Prussians. During the time that it lasts, a new army will be raised, and some fine morning we shall fall upon them again. We shall be ready, and we have a hostage—let us remain here."

We fixed our quarters there. It was terribly cold, and we did not go out much, and somebody had always to keep the female prisoner in sight.

She was sullen, and never said anything, or else spoke of her husband, whom the captain had killed. She looked at him continually with fierce eyes, and we felt that she was tortured by a wild longing for revenge. That seemed to us to be the most suitable punishment for the terrible torments that she had made Piedelot suffer, for impotent vengeance is such intense pain!

Alas! we who knew how to avenge our comrade ought to have thought that this woman would know how to avenge her husband, and have been on our guard. It is true that one of us kept watch every night, and that at first we tied her by a long rope to the great oak bench that was fastened to the wall. But, by and by, as she had never tried to escape, in spite of her hatred for us, we relaxed our extreme prudence, and allowed her to sleep somewhere else except on the bench, and without being tied. What had we to fear? She was at the end of the room, a man was on guard at the door, and between her and the sentinel the captain's wife and two other men used to lie. She was alone and unarmed against four, so there could be no danger.

One night when we were asleep, and the captain was on guard, the lancer's wife was lying more quietly in her corner than usual, and she had even smiled for the first time since she had been our prisoner during the evening. Suddenly, however, in the middle of the night, we were all awakened by a terrible cry. We got up, groping about, and at once stumbled over a furious couple who were rolling about and fighting on the ground. It was the captain and the lancer's wife. We threw ourselves on them, and separated them in a moment. She was shouting and laughing, and he seemed to have the death rattle. All this took place in the dark. Two of us held her, and when a light was struck a terrible sight met our eyes. The captain was lying on the floor in a pool of blood, with an enormous gash in his throat, and his sword bayonet, that had been taken from his rifle, was sticking in the red, gaping wound. A few minutes afterward he died, without having been able to utter a word.

His wife did not shed a tear. Her eyes were dry, her throat was contracted, and she looked at the lancer's wife steadfastly, and with a calm ferocity that inspired fear.

"This woman belongs to me," she said to us suddenly. "You swore to me not a week ago to let me kill her as I chose, if she killed my husband; and you must keep your oath. You must fasten her securely to the fireplace, upright against the back of it, and then you can go where you like, but far from here. I will take my revenge on her myself. Leave the captain's body, and we three, he, she and I, will remain here."

We obeyed, and went away. She promised to write to us to Geneva, as we were returning thither.

VI

Two days later I received the following letter, dated the day after we had left, that had been written at an inn on the high road:

"MY FRIEND: I am writing to you, according to my promise. For the moment I am at the inn, where I have just handed my prisoner over to a Prussian officer.

"I must tell you, my friend, that this poor woman has left two children in Germany. She had followed her husband, whom she adored, as she did not wish him to be exposed to the risks of war by himself, and as her children were with their grandparents. I have learned all this since yesterday, and it has turned my ideas of vengeance into more humane feelings. At the very moment when I felt pleasure in insulting this woman, and in threatening her with the most fearful torments, in recalling Piedelot, who had been burned alive, and in threatening her with a similar death, she looked at me coldly, and said:

"'What have you got to reproach me with, Frenchwoman? You think that you will do right in avenging your husband's death, is not that so?'

"'Yes,' I replied.

"'Very well, then; in killing him, I did what you are going to do in burning me. I avenged my husband, for your husband killed him.'

"'Well,' I replied, 'as you approve of this vengeance, prepare to endure it.'

"'I do not fear it.'

"And in fact she did not seem to have lost courage. Her face was calm, and she looked at me without trembling, while I brought wood and dried leaves together, and feverishly threw on to them the powder from some cartridges, which was to make her funeral pile the more cruel.

"I hesitated in my thoughts of persecution for a moment. But the captain was there, pale and covered with blood, and he seemed to be looking at me with his large, glassy eyes, and I applied myself to my work again after kissing his pale lips. Suddenly, however, on raising my head, I saw that she was crying, and I felt rather surprised.

"'So you are frightened?' I said to her.

"'No, but when I saw you kiss your husband, I thought of mine, of all whom I love.'

"She continued to sob, but stopping suddenly, she said to me in broken words and in a low voice:

"'Have you any children?'

"A shiver rare over me, for I guessed that this poor woman had some. She asked me to look in a pocketbook which was in her bosom, and in it I saw two photographs of quite young children, a boy and a girl, with those kind, gentle, chubby faces that German children have. In it there were also two locks of light hair and a letter in a large, childish hand, and beginning with German words which meant:

"'My dear little mother.

"'I could not restrain my tears, my dear friend, and so I untied her, and without venturing to look at the face of my poor dead husband, who was not to be avenged, I went with her as far as the inn. She is free; I have just left her, and she kissed me with tears. I am going upstairs to my husband; come as soon as possible, my dear friend, to look for our two bodies.'"

I set off with all speed, and when I arrived there was a Prussian patrol at the cottage; and when I asked what it all meant, I was told that there was a captain of francs-tireurs and his wife inside, both dead. I gave their names; they saw that I knew them, and I begged to be allowed to arrange their funeral.

"Somebody has already undertaken it," was the reply. "Go in if you wish to, as you know them. You can settle about their funeral with their friend."

I went in. The captain and his wife were lying side by side on a bed, and were covered by a sheet. I raised it, and saw that the woman had inflicted a similar wound in her throat to that from which her husband had died.

At the side of the bed there sat, watching and weeping, the woman who had been mentioned to me as their best friend. It was the lancer's wife.

Printed in Great Britain
by Amazon